the **BAD GUYS**

in

ONE
LAST
THING

MR. WOLF

TEXT AND ILLUSTRATIONS COPYRIGHT © 2024 BY AARON BLABEY

ISBN 978-1-5461-1180-1

10 9 8 7 6 5 4 3 2 1   24 25 26 27 28

PRINTED IN THE U.S.A.   132
FIRST U.S. PRINTING 2024

· AARON BLABEY ·

the BAD GUYS

in

ONE
LAST
THING

SCHOLASTIC INC.

This one'll make us famous . . .

Yeah.
Whaddya say?
Ready to become a

LEGEND,

buddy?

Twenty-one banks today!

Whaddya mean
you don't like cake?

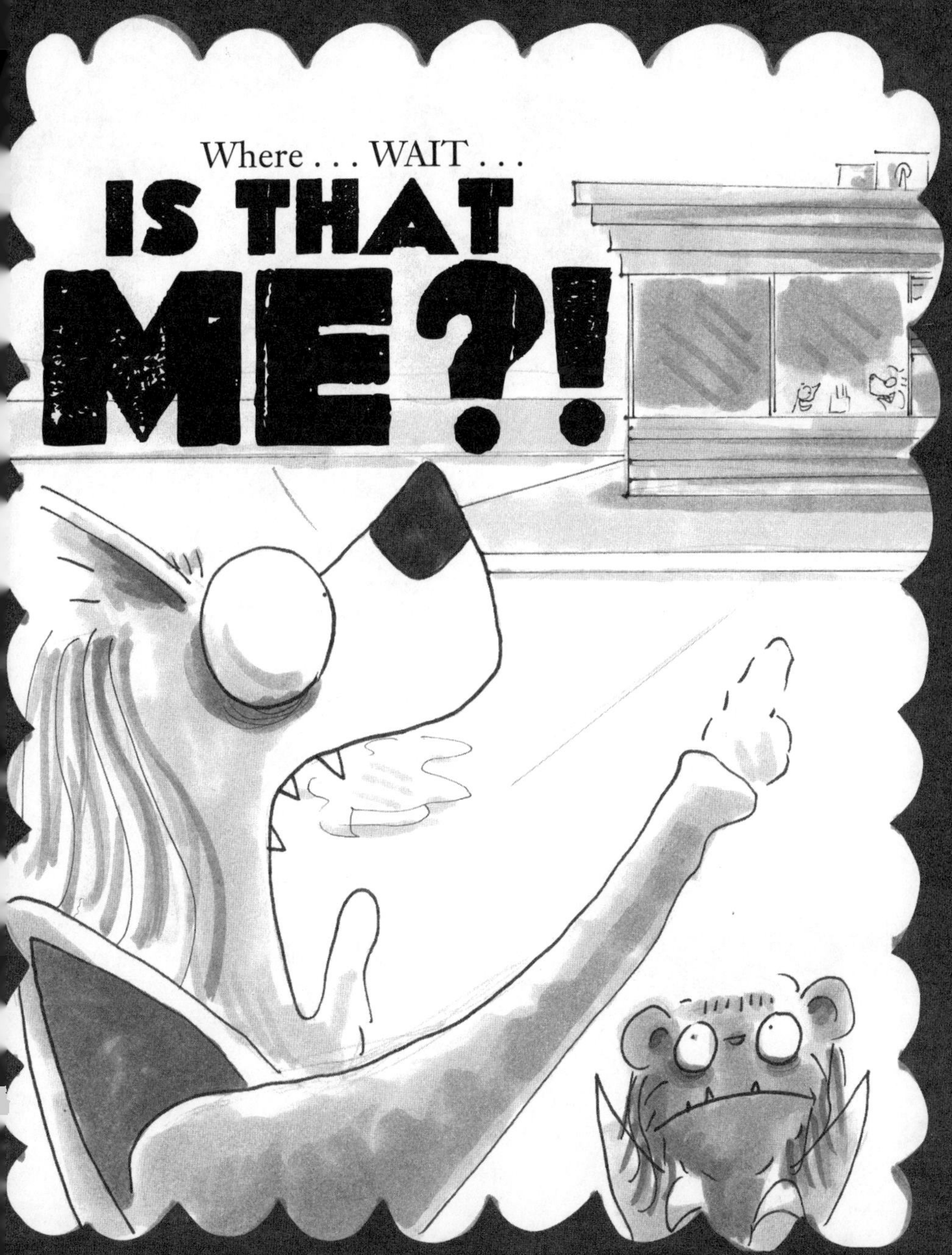
Where . . . WAIT . . .
IS THAT ME?!

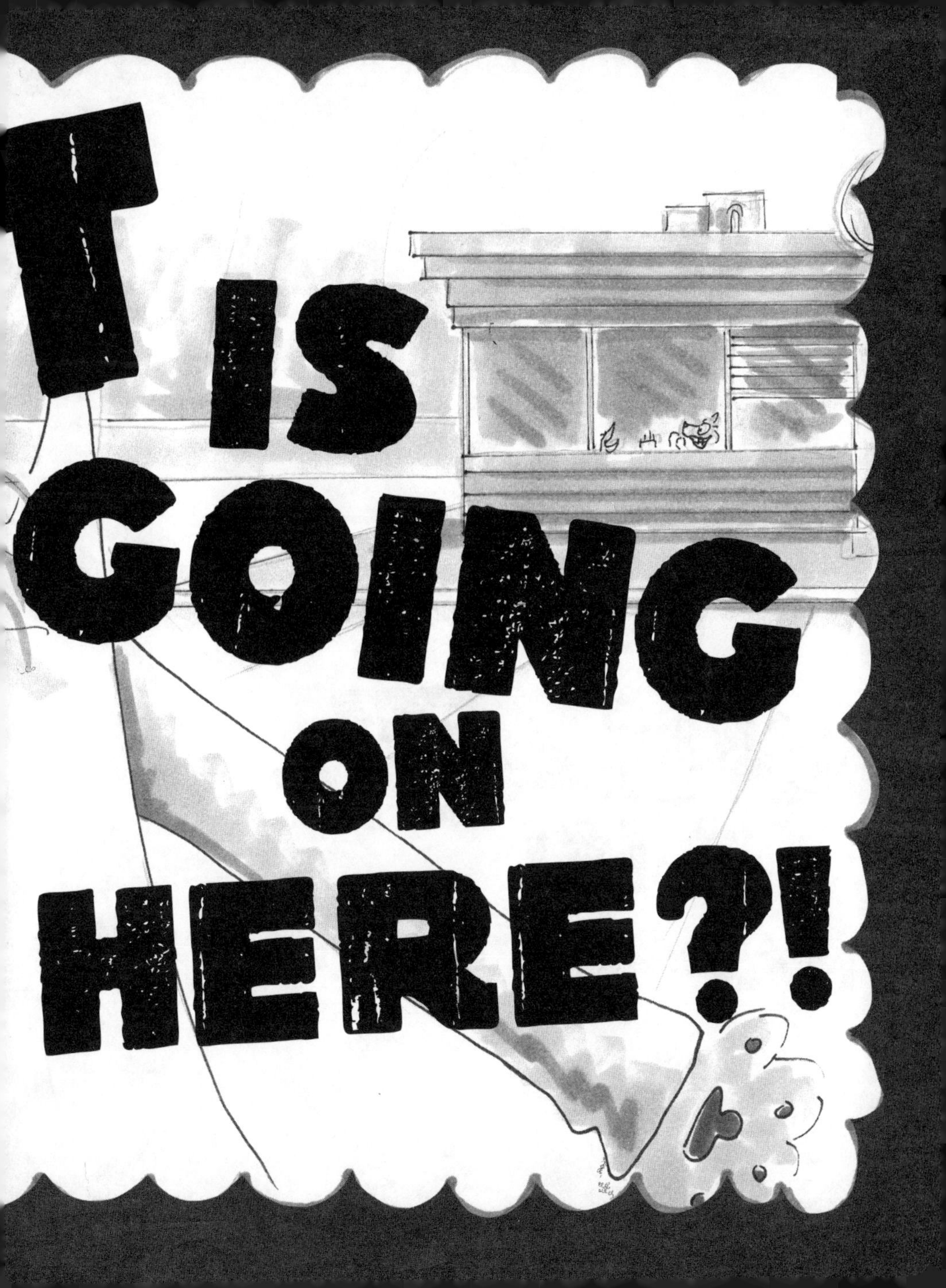
T IS GOING ON HERE?!

· CHAPTER 1 ·
FIRST DAY AT SCHOOL

I MEAN . . . THAT'S **ME!** HOW AM I **WATCHING MYSELF?!**

Hmmm.
Well, if your
life was a series,
you could think of
this book as a
FLASHBACK.

The edges of the frame
might even be

BUMPY

like a cloud

to

SHOW

that it's a flashback . . .

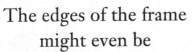

That would be a simple
but effective idea . . .

But WAIT!
Even IF my life was
a series, I wouldn't be
able to go back and

BE INVOLVED

in a flashback.

That's not how flashbacks work.

Aren't you forgetting
something?

SPACE AND TIME
have no power over me.

I can go to
ANY PLACE.

I can go to
ANY TIME.

And now . . . *so can you.*

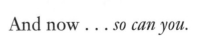

WE TIME-TRAVELED?!

Yes.

We've actually **TRAVELED INTO THE** *PAST?!*

This is **ACTUALLY ME**, visiting **MYSELF**, in the **PAST?!**

You've got it.

In fact, if your life **WAS** a series,
the frames wouldn't *really* need
bumpy edges now because it

TECHNICALLY

wouldn't be a flashback

anymore because

THIS

is where

YOU
ACTUALLY
ARE.

That's SO confusing.

You'll get used to it.

Wait . . .

What am I
WEARING?!

You don't like it?

AND WHAT'S UP
WITH MY

HAIR?!

Enough questions.
We have an important job to do.

ENOUGH QUESTIONS?!

One minute I was fighting a

GIANT CENTIPEDE

and then,

WITHOUT WARNING,

I've somehow

TRAVELED THROUGH TIME

to visit

MYSELF

sitting in a diner with Snake.

I HAVE NOT ASKED ENOUGH QUESTIONS!

Alright.
I'll give you a quick

TIME-TRAVEL
DEMONSTRATION.

Just a quick one.
And then
we need to get to work.

Work?
What work?
What are you talking about?!

And why are you a
TASMANIAN DEVIL
again?!
Why aren't you a
BLOB OF
WHITE LIGHT
with a little face
and a mullet . . . ?

Wait!
Do *I* have a
MULLET?!

I'm a Tasmanian devil because that *draws less attention.*

And you have the
SACRED HAIR . . .

. . . because YOU are my new
APPRENTICE.

I'm sorry . . . *WHAT?!*

Let me show you.

click!

FLASH!

· CHAPTER 2 ·
NOT DEAD YET

A GHOST! GET BACK, DIABLO! GET BACK!

Wolf?
Is that you . . . ?

Hey, big guy.

DON'T SPEAK TO IT, HERMANO! DON'T LOOK IT IN THE EYES!

Piranha, it's *me* . . .

I DO NOT FEAR YOU!

CHICO!
WHAT ARE YOU DOING?!

It's really you.

After we beat the Centipede,
I got zapped back into the

PAST.

And now
I've been zapped
back to the . . . *ahem* . . .

FUTURE.

Just to say HI!

Is that right?

Yep.

YOU CAN TALK?!

Long story.

I told you it was
too early
for a funeral . . .

You OK?

Yeah.
Confused.
But OK.

YOU!

One day soon,
you're going to tell me

EVERYTHING.

Right?

I know.
I owe you an explanation.

You know you do.

You've been busy

SAVING THE WORLD?

Nah, sugar.
We **RETIRED.**
Isn't that right, baby?

Yeah.
We're going to travel the world.
Help those who need it.
I've dusted off my

MEDICAL DEGREE.

And this one is secretly a

**QUALIFIED
ENGINEER.**

I'm all *that*.

We're going to make
a difference.
After all the other stuff,
that sounds like a holiday,
doesn't it?

But who's
going
to keep the
world safe
without you?

WE
ARE!

If it isn't Mr. Wolf!

We all agreed . . .

TOO EARLY FOR A FUNERAL.

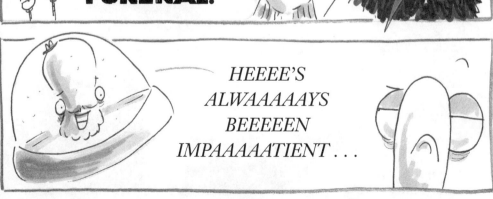

HEEEE'S ALWAAAAAYS BEEEEEN IMPAAAAATIENT . . .

You guys look
AMAZING!

Thank you,
Mr. Wolf.

And what have you come as?

OK, PEEPS!

WE GOTTA GO!

We have a multiverse
to protect, remember?

It was good
to see you, Mr. Wolf.

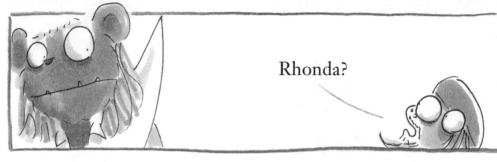

Rhonda?

Is he . . . with you?

I'm always here, dear boy.

And I'm SO proud of who you've become.

C'mon, buddy. There's trouble in

QUADRANT 9.

We gotta hustle.

Yeah!
Move it, buddy!

Who asked you?

Sorry! My bad!

Whatever.
OK, RAMBLERS!
**LET'S GET
RAMBLIN'** . . .

On my way . . .

See you, Milt!

And you, too, Wolfie.
I knew you weren't dead.

We gotta split, too.
It was good to see
you, buddy.

EXPLANATION.

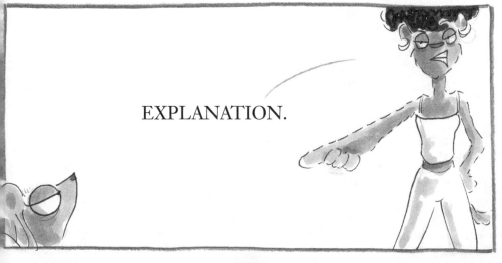

Is . . .

She's right up there.

You've got a job to do, Wolf.

Can't I just say hi?

Five minutes.

If you can control **SPACE** and **TIME**, why are you in such a *hurry*?

I'm PUNCTUAL.

Do you have to take medication for that?

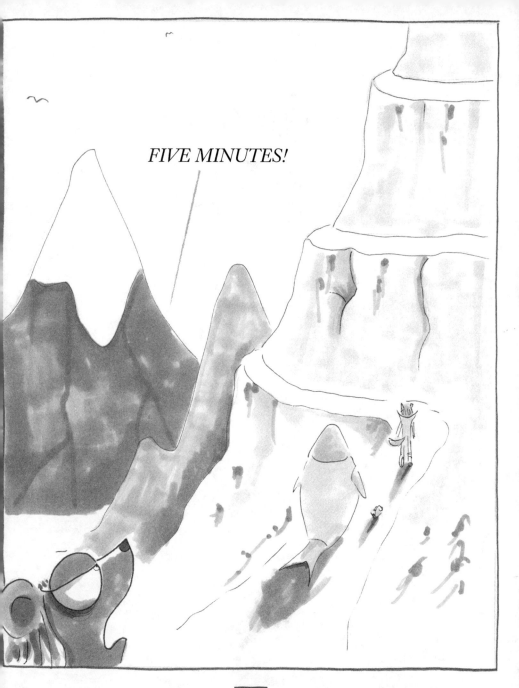

FIVE MINUTES!

· CHAPTER 3 ·
HER

OK. That's lunch.
Get out of here.

And stay out
of trouble!

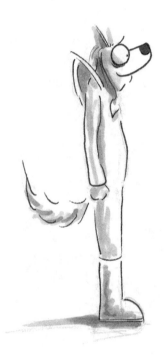

What did we tell you?

IT SEEMED LIKE HE WAS DEAD!

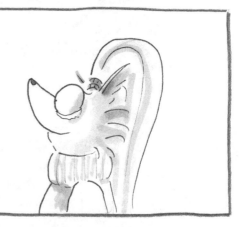

You taking
good care of him?

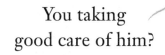

Whaddya think?

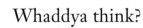

Are you . . .
OK, Ellen?

Yeah, I'm doing good.
Feeling better every day.

Are you . . .

Retired?

Yeah, the **B-TEAM'S** killing it.

But . . .

What am I doing with myself?

You always know what I'm about to say . . .

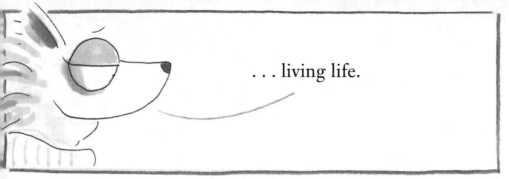

. . . living life.

That was so brave.
    What you did.

It had to be done.

You were
pretty brave
yourself.

And now look at you!

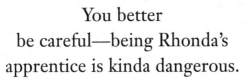

You better
be careful—being Rhonda's
apprentice is kinda dangerous.

She keeps telling me
we have to leave.
That I have
"a job to do."

Hmmm.
I wonder what
that could be.

Ellen?

Yeah, Wolfie?

You really are my hero.

And you're mine,
Mr. Wolf.

Follow me.

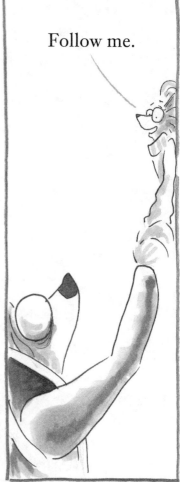

Up there.

I'll see you
in a minute.

We told him
you weren't dead.

· CHAPTER 4 ·
HIM

It's you.

Yeah,
it's me.

How you feeling?

COUGH!
COUGH!

Can't complain.
You?

Pretty good.
For a freaked-out
time-traveler with
a mullet.

I wasn't going to
mention the hair . . .

It's OK.
Knock yourself
out.

Nah . . .
looks good!

COUGH!

COUGH!

COUGH!

You sure you're feeling OK?

But I can still feel it.
Deep inside.
It feels like . . .

. . . poison.

I did terrible things, buddy.

It wasn't you. You were being controlled . . .

THAT'S NO EXCUSE.

I should have been stronger.

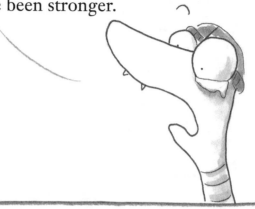

If I'd been half the guy you are,
none of this would have
happened.

You really
like my hair?

Nah.
You look crazy.

Thanks, Ellen.

Yeah.
Sounds good.

Oh, and **JOY**
said to tell you—
she'll be back by
tomorrow morning
so you two won't miss
your
**MOVIE
DAY.**

Ah, great.
We're doing a
**ROMANTIC
COMEDY**
marathon.

Who are you
and what have
you done with
Mr. Snake?

New and improved, buddy.
New and improved.

It's time.

It's OK.
We're not going anywhere.
You can visit us anytime.

Literally!

KISS!

Well, if you think
you're getting a kiss from me,
you're outta your mind.

Time for work, Mr. Wolf.

Always so mysterious.

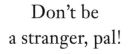

Don't be
a stranger, pal!

Yeah, *chico*!
Come home soon!

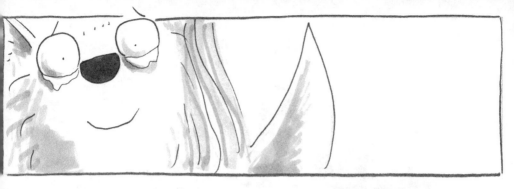

· CHAPTER 5 ·

THE
PARADOX

And . . . *here we are again.*

WHY DID YOU
DECIDE TO
GO GOOD?

What?

Well, if you imagine your life was a series,
in **BOOK ONE**, you decided to
STOP BEING BAD.

That means there must
have been a moment when
you said to yourself,
"I don't want to be the

BIG BAD
WOLF

anymore."

There must have been a moment when you said, "I don't want to be scary anymore.

I WANT TO BE GOOD."

How did that *happen?*

I just . . . called the guys and told them we were going to go GOOD.

But do you remember **WHY?**

Because look at THAT guy.

Does **HE** look like he wants to *go good*?

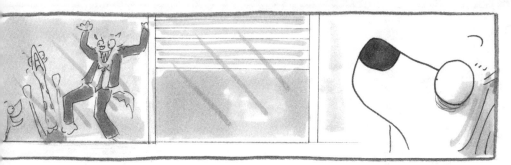

No . . .
he really doesn't . . .

But if he **DOESN'T** go good, the multiverse is in a lot of trouble, isn't it?

Yeah . . .

So?

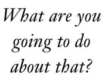
What are you going to do about that?

Are you saying . . .

I NEED
TO TELL
MYSELF
(my old self)
TO BE GOOD
or . . .

HE
WON'T
GO
GOOD?!

That's what
I'm saying.

But that
doesn't make any sense . . .

It's a
PARADOX.

Do you need
to take medication
for that?

You need to **GET IN THERE** and convince

YOUR OLD SELF TO CHANGE HIS WAYS.

But if

THAT

is why I went good—

if I changed my ways because a version of myself from the future came by and told me to—

WHY CAN'T I REMEMBER THAT?!

I gave you **SPECIAL POWERS,** remember? Perhaps they have something to do with it.

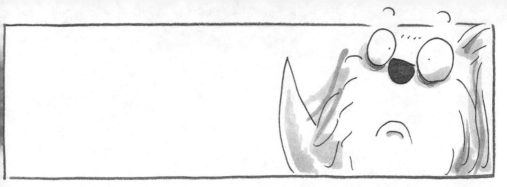

Oh, LOOK!

See you, buddy.
Happy twenty-first!

This is your chance.

GET IN THERE!

· CHAPTER 6 ·
WOLVES

Garçon!
More coffee!

And there's no
easy way to say this . . .

. . . I'm from the
FUTURE.

Right.

Check, please!

NO!
Look at me!
I mean . . .
LOOK AT
YOURSELF!

It's ME!

YOU!

I mean . . .

Is there something wrong with my coffee?

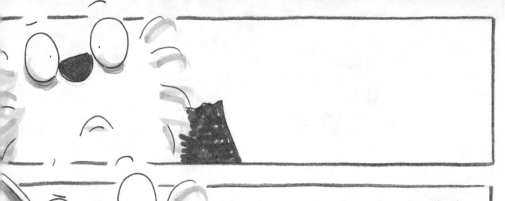

I'm sorry . . . *what?*

YOU NEED TO
**STOP
BEING
BAD!**

. . . stop being bad . . .

YES!

STOP
BEING
BAD?

YES!

OK, that's *very* good . . .

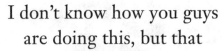

I don't know how you guys
are doing this, but that
MASK
is very, very good.
BRAVO!
Snake?
Come on out! *You got me!*
Oh man, you
GOT me . . .

It's not a mask.

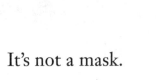

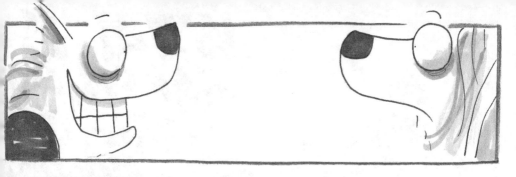

Listen . . . It's very simple.

STOP BEING BAD

or the

UNIVERSE WILL BE DESTROYED.

First by

ALIENS with BUTT HANDS

and then by an

ANCIENT CENTIPEDE

who turns

SNAKE

into a

SUPER-VILLAIN.

Maybe even a
WILDLY
SUCCESSFUL
ANIMATED
MOVIE!

OK . . .
This has been great,
but I have to go now . . .

. . . my powers.

I wonder . . .

Do you believe me?

Yes.

OK, then listen—when I click my fingers,

YOU'LL GO TO SLEEP.

And when you wake up, you won't remember

ANY OF THIS.

But you will know

ONE THING.

• CHAPTER 7 •
REFORMED CHARACTER

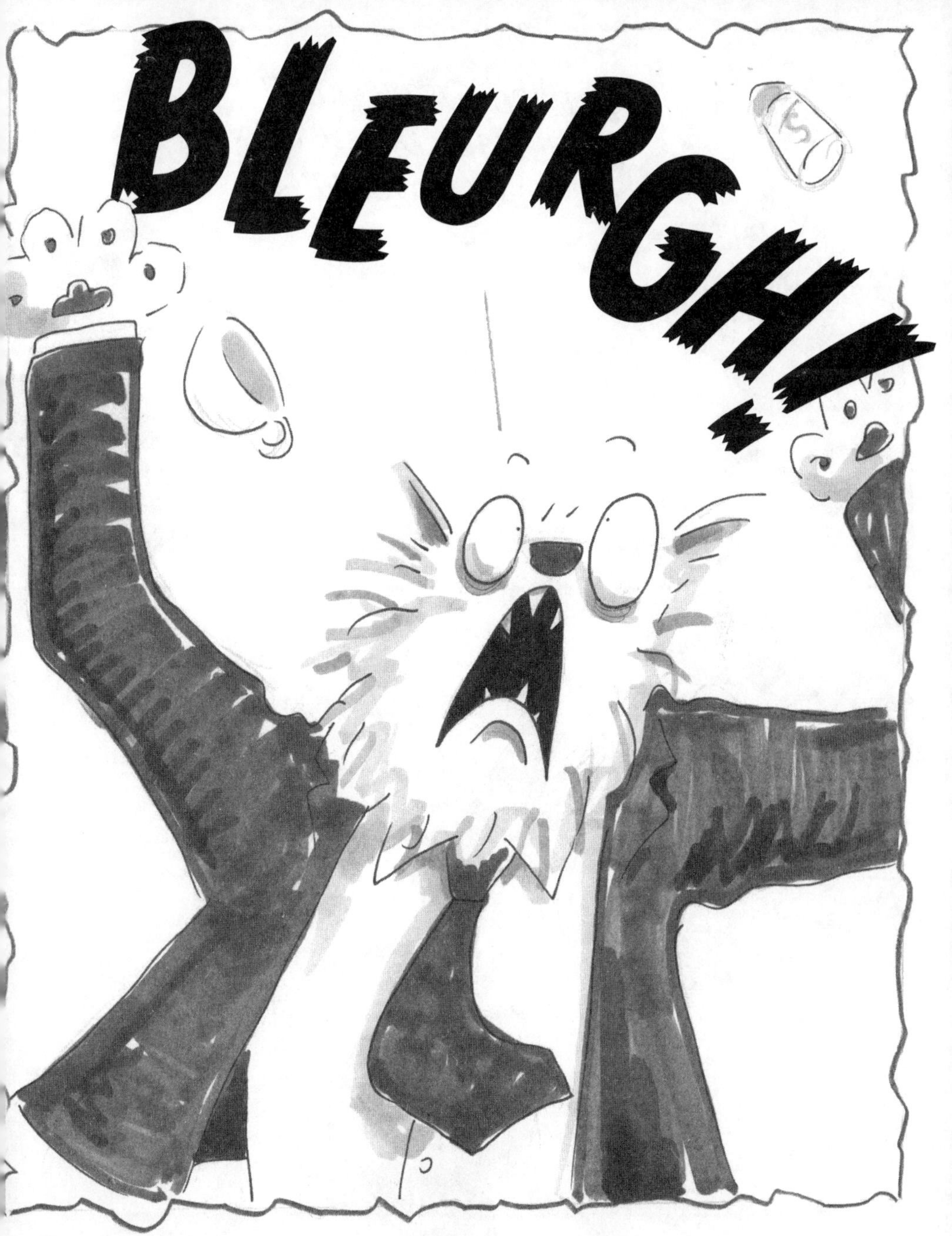
BLEURGH!!

I'm not a bad . . . GUY.

. . . heh heh . . .

REALLY!

I gotta go.

I need to . . .
START A CLUB!

The **GOOD GUYS CLUB!**

That's a terrible name . . .

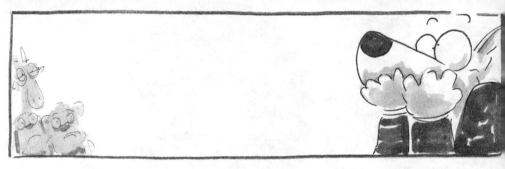

Y'all have a great day.

· CHAPTER 8 ·
GOOD.
BYE.

Heeey! Look who it is!
It's my good pal,

MR. SNAKE.

You're going to *love* him.
He's a real . . .

sweetheart.

You got any mice?

IT WORKED!

Well, well. If it isn't

MR.
PIRANHA.

Hola.

So . . .
NOW WHAT?

So where's the MEAT?

Well, the multiverse is a big place.

I could use some help
taking care of it.

There are a lot of

BAD
GUYS

out there . . .

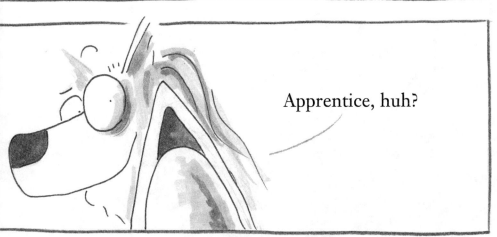

Yep.

And this is kind of **DANGEROUS**, yeah?

Could be.

Let's go do some GOOD!

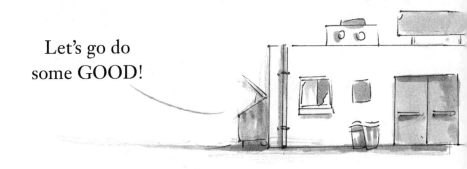

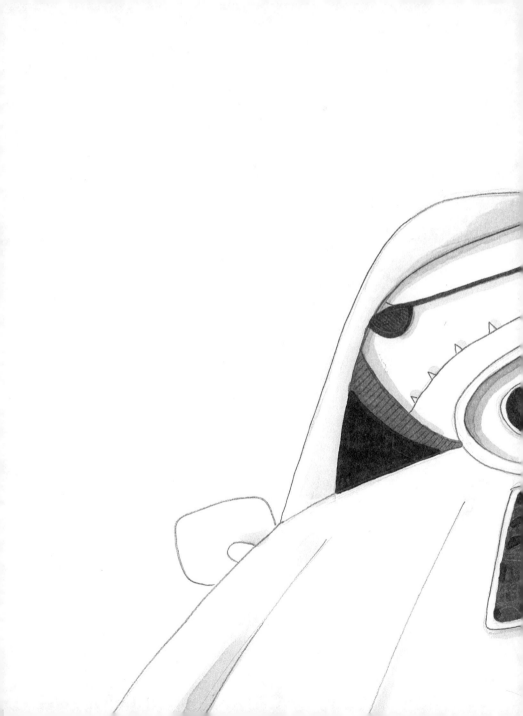

THE

END.

THE EN
ME

But what about ME

If this was a series, I would

and everyone would want

to know what

happened to ME

I'M SO INTERESTING

AND BEGUILING!

AND TOTALLY HOT!

WHAT WERE THEY
THINKING?!

D?
EEEEE?!
be the STAR
EEEEEEE!
F THIS WAS
A SERIES,
THIS
COULDN'T
POSSIBLY
BE THE END!

IT

IS.

TO ALL THE FANS—
WE LOVE YOU.

the **BAD**
GUYS
(and A.B.)